GIVE ME BACK MY DAD!

GIVE ME BACK MY DAD!

Robert Munsch

illustrated by
Michael Martchenko

Scholastic Canada Ltd.
Toronto   New York   London Auckland Sydney
Mexico City New Delhi Hong Kong Buenos Aires

Scholastic Canada Ltd.
604 King Street West, Toronto, Ontario M5V 1E1, Canada

Scholastic Inc.
557 Broadway, New York, NY 10012, USA

Scholastic Australia Pty Limited
PO Box 579, Gosford, NSW 2250, Australia

Scholastic New Zealand Limited
Private Bag 94407, Botany, Manukau 2163, New Zealand

Scholastic Children's Books
Euston House, 24 Eversholt Street, London NW1 1DB, UK

The illustrations in this book were painted in watercolour
on illustration board.
The type is set in Cambria Regular.

Library and Archives Canada Cataloguing in Publication
Munsch, Robert N., 1945-

Give me back my dad! / Robert Munsch ; illustrated by Michael
Martchenko.

ISBN 978-1-4431-0764-8

I. Martchenko, Michael II. Title.

PS8576.U575G58 2011   jC813'.54   C2011-901801-2

6 5 4 3 2 1   Printed in Canada 114   11 12 13 14 15

To Cheryl Shiwak,
Rigolet, Labrador.
—R.M.

One day, Cheryl and her father decided to go ice fishing. They got on the snowmobile, put all their stuff in the sled on the back, and went bouncing over bumps and across lakes until they came to a very good place to fish.

"This place," said Cheryl's father, "is the best place to fish in the whole world. But the fish are smart. You've got to be really smart to catch these fish."

"Phooey!" said Cheryl. "I'm smarter than any fish."

So her father got out an ice drill and drilled an enormous hole. They chopped the ice and drilled some more, and then they were done.

"WOW!" said Cheryl's father. "Really thick ice! Now we can fish!"

He got out a hook and line and bait and said to Cheryl, "You fish down this hole, but be very careful because these fish are smart."

"Phooey!" said Cheryl. "I'm smarter than any fish."

She jigged her line
up and *down* and
    up and *down* and
        up and *down* and
            up and *down*
and said, "I want to catch a fish."

"Be patient," said her dad.

So Cheryl jigged her line
up and *down* and
    up and *down* and
        up and *down* and
            up and *down*
and said, "I want to catch a fish."

Then up out of the hole came a candy bar with a line on it.

"Look at that!" said Cheryl. "It's a candy bar."

Her father yelled,

"DON'T TOUCH THAT!"

But Cheryl grabbed the candy bar and was pulled right down underneath the ice.

Cheryl's father yelled down the hole,
"Give me back my baby!"

A big fish stuck its head out of the water and said, "We caught this kid fair and square. You can't have her back."

"Grrrrr," said Cheryl's father.

Cheryl's father got an idea. He put
a very small piece of bait on a line and
jigged it
 UP and *down* and
　　 UP and *down* and
　　　 UP and *down* and
　　　　 UP and *down*

and all of a sudden he pulled up a very
small baby fish.

The big fish stuck its head out of the
water and said, ***"Give me back my baby!"***

"Well," said Cheryl's father, "I'll give you
back YOUR baby if you will give me back
MY baby."

"Grrrrr," said the big fish.

Cheryl's father tossed the little fish back and Cheryl came flying up out of the hole.

She said, "Brrrrrrrrr, it's cold," and right away she started turning into an icicle.

Her father picked her up, ran to shore and got a fire going in the Labrador tent.

Soon Cheryl was warm and dry like a piece of toast.

"Now," said her father, "we are going back out there. Don't pick up anything the fish throw out of the hole. These are smart fish."

"Right!" said Cheryl.

They went back out and Cheryl jigged her line

UP and *down* and
    UP and *down* and
        UP and *down* and
            UP and *down*

and said, "I want to catch a fish."

A candy bar with a line on it came up out of the hole.

"Oh no," said Cheryl, "I'm not that dumb."
She jigged her line
up and *down* and
   up and *down* and
      up and *down* and
         up and *down*
and said, "I want to catch a fish."

Up came a bag of popcorn with a line on it.

Cheryl said, "Oh no, I'm not that dumb."
She jigged her line
up and *down* and
   up and *down* and
      up and *down* and
         up and *down*
and said, "I want to catch a fish."

Then up came a television.

"WOW!" said Cheryl. "That looks pretty nice. But I'm not that dumb."

Cheryl jigged her line
up and *down* and
   up and *down* and
      up and *down* and
         up and *down*

and said, "I want to catch a fish."

She waited some more, and up came a $50,000 bill with a line on it.

Her father said, "Fifty thousand dollars!" He grabbed it and got pulled underneath the ice.

"Grrrrr," said Cheryl. She yelled
down the hole,

"Give me back my daddy!"

The baby fish stuck its head up out
of the water and said, "Hey! We caught
him fair and square and you can't have
him back."

Cheryl got an idea. She put a huge piece
of bait on the line and she jigged it
UP and *down* and
UP and *down* and
UP and *down* and
UP and *down*
and said, "I've got to catch a daddy fish."

All of a sudden a big fish grabbed the
bait and Cheryl pulled him in.

The baby fish stuck its head out of the
water and said, *"Give me back my daddy!"*

"Well," said Cheryl, "I'll give you back
YOUR daddy if you give me back MY daddy."
"Grrrr!" said the little fish.

Cheryl threw the daddy fish back into the water and Cheryl's father came flying up out of the hole. He said, "Brrrrrrrrr, it's cold," and started turning into an icicle.

Cheryl pulled her father to the tent and put wood into the stove till he was warm and dry like a piece of toast.

Then Cheryl said, "Daddy, why did you grab the money? I thought you were smarter than a fish."

"I AM smarter than a fish," said her dad. "And I know that YOU are smarter than any fish, and I knew you would get me out. And I still have the money!"

"Right!" said Cheryl, and they went back to town and bought Cheryl her very own snowmobile.